THE
CASE
OF THE
MARMALADE
CAT

THE
CASE
OF THE
MARMALADE
CAT

James Heneghan

Cover by
Carol Wakefield

Scholastic Canada Ltd.

Scholastic Canada Ltd.
123 Newkirk Road, Richmond Hill, Ontario, Canada
L4C 3G5

Scholastic Inc.
730 Broadway, New York, NY 10003, USA

Ashton Scholastic Limited
Private Bag 1, Penrose, Auckland, New Zealand

Ashton Scholastic Pty Limited
PO Box 579, Gosford, NSW 2250, Australia

Scholastic Publications Ltd.
Holly Walk, Leamington Spa, Warwickshire CV32 4LS,
England

Canadian Cataloguing in Publication Data

Heneghan, James, 1930-
    The case of the marmalade cat

ISBN 0-590-73824-0

I. Title.

PS8565.E58C3 1991   jC813'.54   C90-095870-7
PZ7.H45Ca 1991

6 5 4 3 2 1   Printed in Canada   1 2 3 4 5/9
                      Manufactured by Webcom Limited

For Margaux.

Chapter  1

When Clarice O'Brien decided to devote her life to fighting crime the first person she told was her best friend, Sadie Stewart. "I'm starting my very own Detective Agency," she said, "devoted to Fighting Crime and Solving Mysteries. I've made a sign. Come on, I'll show you."

Sadie, accustomed to Clarice's tendency to speak in capitals, was only mildly curious. She followed her friend around to the back of the house, and sure enough, on the door of the garden shed where Mr. O'Brien kept all his tools and seeds and clay pots there was a sign:

O'BRIEN DETECTIVE AGENCY
NO JOB TOO BIG OR TOO SMALL
CLARICE O'BRIEN PROP.

The sign could be clearly seen by anyone passing in the lane.

"I don't remember what PROP. means," admitted Clarice, "but it's always on business signs after a person's name. Makes it official."

"It means proprietor," said Sadie. She was a year younger than Clarice, but she read a lot and was smart, and was also a bit of a know-it-all.

"What's that?"

"Owner. Boss. Chief."

"Then that's me all right," said Clarice.

"And you're a detective." It was a statement.

"Right."

"Clarice, you couldn't detect a Doberman in a duck pond. So where did you get the idea you could be a detective?" Her eyes narrowed accusingly. "You've been reading a book!"

"Not really a book," Clarice protested. "It was a magazine article on this woman who is Chief Detective in Winnipeg. Women," she added loftily, "are doing all kinds of exciting jobs these days — fighting fires, fighting crime, exploring outer space . . ."

Sadie wasn't convinced. "But that's grown-up stuff. You're not a woman, you're just a kid."

"Well, you have to start somewhere, you

know," said Clarice airily, dismissing her friend's argument with a wave of her hand. "Besides, I plan to start reading a whole bunch of books soon, the ones written by Sherlock Holmes, the world-famous detective."

"It wasn't Sherlock Holmes who wrote the books," said Sadie, "everyone knows that. It was Dr. Watson. Anyway," she pointed out, "what's the good of a sign that can only be seen from the back lane?"

"You'd be surprised," said Clarice. "Thousands of people use the back lane. This is my office. If you don't ask any more dumb questions you can come in and see what I've done." She led the way inside and stood proudly as Sadie inspected the potting table which had been cleared to make a desk under the window. On the desk was a small notebook, a pencil holder containing several sharp pencils, a desk calendar and a magnifying glass which had a slight chip out of its lower edge near the handle. There were two wooden chairs, one pushed under the desk, and one placed beside it. Clarice pointed to the second chair. "That's where I interview Clients."

"What clients?"

"People who hire me to detect things for

them," said Clarice patiently.

Sadie scowled. "Everyone knows what clients are. I meant what clients have you had?"

Clarice didn't seem to have heard her. "Then I go out," she continued enthusiastically, "and I Solve Cases and become a World-Famous Detective."

"Solve what cases?"

"Crimes, mysteries," said Clarice, "what else?"

"You mean you've had clients already?"

"No, not yet, but they'll be coming soon once they've seen my sign, you can bet on that. Which is why I've got a calendar, to make appointments, so they won't all come at once. Besides, I'll only be able to handle one or two cases at a time. The rest will have to wait until I get time to solve them."

"But what do you know about solving crimes?" said Sadie.

"You'd be surprised," said Clarice darkly. "I get hunches. It's a natural ability. Call it a Sixth Sense if you like. I get a feeling about things sometimes. For instance, take the time my bike went missing from outside Blunt's Bakery. I got a burning sensation . . . "

"From eating too many hot cinnamon buns," interrupted Sadie.

Clarice's frown was meant as a warning to her friend. " . . . and I knew somehow, in some mysterious way, that it was rotten Bob Bream who took it."

"You knew 'cause rotten Bob Bream steals everyone's bike," said Sadie. "Besides, you found your bike in the back lane behind the Breams'. I don't call that a sixth sense hunch. Bet I could solve crimes just as well. I would use my superior reasoning powers."

"Well, I use Reasoning Powers too," admitted Clarice. "But when they don't work, I've got my keenly developed Sixth Sense to fall back on."

Sadie was beginning to look impressed. "Do you think I could be a detective too, Clarice? I'd be really useful. As well as my superior reasoning powers I've got very powerful ears. Sometimes I can hear things a mile away. Yesterday, for instance, my mother said to Mrs. Prendergast, 'Keep your voice down, Veronica, Sadie is in the kitchen. She can hear things through walls. She's got ears like a giant rabbit.' And it's true. Even though they were whispering I could hear them talking about the new lady in the florist's shop and how she'd been making eyes at the bank manager, Mr. Samson. As if I cared, but I've got powerful hearing and no mistake."

Clarice considered. "I dunno, Sadie. Tell you what. You could be my secretary, and then we could see if you have any powers I could use. Later, if things work out, I might promote you to the rank of Detective. Then you'd be the same as me only lower, OK?"

Sadie looked disappointed. "Secretary? All a secretary does is write reports and letters."

"Why, a secretary is real important. Detectives couldn't solve anything without secretaries. They take vital notes and stuff like that. When I interview Clients and Criminals you take it all down in shorthand. Think of all the interesting people you'll meet."

"I don't know any shorthand, only longhand."

"Longhand is better really," said Clarice. "You get more written down with longhand."

Sadie was unsure. "Well, I don't know, Clarice, seems to me you get all the interesting jobs, talking to criminals and such. I just get the boring things."

"You gotta start at the bottom," said Clarice. "Everyone starts at the bottom."

Sadie finally agreed to be secretary on one condition: that she be allowed to become a full detective when they had solved their first case.

"OK," said Clarice. "Now all we have to do is wait for our first Client."

They waited. Sadie slouched in the client's chair and read a book called *Witches and Warlocks*. Clarice tidied up the shed a little more by stacking seed catalogues and bric-a-brac high up on the shelves out of the way.

But nobody came.

"It's boring in the garden shed," said Sadie, "and this chair is hard. Let's go for an ice cream. I've got two dollars."

"We gotta be here for when we're needed," said Clarice. "On Duty. What would happen if Clients rushed over here with Crimes to Solve and we were out enjoying ourselves? And it's not a garden shed, it's a Detective Agency."

"Why not write our hours of business on the sign?" suggested Sadie. "Then we wouldn't have to be here all the time. And we could nail one of those empty coffee cans on the door so people — clients — could leave messages inside. Like a mailbox. We could leave paper and a pencil inside too. Then it's like we're always on duty even when we're not here."

Clarice had to admit it was a good idea. She handed a pen to Sadie. "OK, write some office hours on the sign. I'll nail the coffee can up and you can write 'Messages' on it."

When they had finished they stood back to admire their handiwork. Sadie had written:

HOURS

WEEKENDS. 10 TO 6

WEEKDAYS. 4 TO 6

"There, that's it," said Sadie, "let's go."

When they got back there were no messages in the coffee can.

Chapter 2

The next day was Thursday. After school they made themselves comfortable in the Agency office and waited.

Just before five o'clock there was a knock on the door. When Sadie opened it a thin boy with spiky yellow hair said, "You O'Brien?" He held the handlebar of his bicycle carelessly in one hand.

"No." Sadie jerked a thumb at Clarice. "It is she."

The boy allowed the bicycle to slip from his hand so that it bumped to a gentle rest against the shed wall. He sauntered in.

Clarice was sitting behind her desk. "What

can I do for you?" She waved the boy towards the second chair but he ignored it.

"You the chief of this detective agency?" He spoke very quietly, as though talking were an effort.

"That's right, I'm Clarice O'Brien. This is my secretary. Her name is Sadie."

"I need a job," said the boy, "as a detective."

"We don't need anybody right now. No openings," said Clarice.

"No cases either," said Sadie.

The boy ignored Sadie. He continued to stare at Clarice, his strange amber-coloured eyes serious and unblinking. "You see these hands and feet?"

The two girls stared at his thin bony hands thrust out in front of his chest like claws.

"Deadly weapons," explained the boy.

His movements up to now had been fluid and gracefully casual, like those of a sleepy cat. But now he exploded into action, slashing at the empty air with his hands and feet.

"Aaargh!" he screamed.

The girls fell back in alarm.

The boy relaxed again. In his slow, drawling voice he said, "Also, I've had experience."

Clarice was the first to recover. "What experience have you had?"

"Solved a crime at school."

"What crime?" said Sadie.

"Somebody stole Melinda Appleby's pencil case and she asked me to find it for her and I did."

"Who's Melinda Appleby?" said Sadie.

The boy weighed the question carefully. "Girl who sits behind me in Miss Plum's class."

"What happened to the girl who stole it?" said Sadie.

The questions were too fast and too many. The boy scratched his yellow head. "Wasn't a girl. It was Gordie Grilse. I punched him out."

"Then what?" said Sadie.

"Melinda Appleby gave me her peanut butter sandwich."

Clarice studied the strange boy from the tips of his spiky yellow hair to the soles of his tattered sneakers. There was a sun-baked, tawny look about him, and his face was covered with freckles the same colour as his eyes. If you wanted to paint him, all you'd need would be yellows and golds. Clarice said, "Why does your hair stick up all over like that?"

The boy shrugged. "Same reason your red

hair glows like a bushfire." He thought for a while, then jerked his thumb over at Sadie. "And why she got buck teeth with chrome fenders."

"I don't have buck teeth," said Sadie indignantly, "just a slight overbite. Which is why I have to wear these braces. And besides," she added, "they're only temporary."

"And my hair's not red," said Clarice haughtily, "it's titian."

The boy said no more. He stared at Clarice unblinkingly with those amber eyes.

"You could be useful in a tough spot maybe," allowed Clarice. "You've got a good build."

"Like a popsicle stick," murmured Sadie.

The boy squared his thin shoulders. "Do I get the job?"

"What do you think, Sadie? Can we use him?"

Sadie pushed her long brown hair back out of her eyes. "He's a bit mouthy." She pulled a face. "But he looks OK. If he punched out Gordon Grilse he must be pretty good."

"OK, you're on, so long as you understand there's no pay unless we get a Client who comes up with the cash," said Clarice. "What's your name?"

He was a long time answering. At last he

said, "Call me Brick."

Clarice shook his bony hand. Then Sadie shook it too.

"When do I start?" said Brick.

"Tomorrow. Be here soon as you can after school," said Clarice. "I'm expecting a Case any time now."

Brick nodded and left without another word.

Clarice and Sadie watched out the window as he rode his bike down the back lane. They continued watching until his spiky yellow head had disappeared into the October twilight.

Chapter  3

The next day no clients came to the O'Brien Detective Agency.

Until just as they were about to close.

Clarice, pretending to be busy with her arithmetic homework, was actually composing a notice for the supermarket notice board informing shoppers that the O'Brien Detective Agency was now in business. "We gotta advertise," she explained to Sadie.

Sadie, sitting in the second chair, was reading as usual. Sadie was always reading. She carried a book with her everywhere, jammed into the pocket of her expensive denim jacket. The light from the small 40-watt bulb hanging from the ceiling wasn't good and she had to tilt the book occasionally to see the small print.

Brick was collapsed on the top of a sack of seed potatoes, thumbing idly through a seed catalogue and making strange breathing noises through his nostrils as he jabbed his elbows into the potato sack.

It was almost six o'clock. Sadie stretched and yawned. "This is too much excitement for me. I'm going home."

Suddenly there came a loud and startling rattle at the door.

Sadie stiffened. "What was that?"

"Sounded like the coffee can," said Clarice. She walked to the door and reached for the latch.

Brick slid off his potato sack. Sadie backed away from the door.

Clarice pulled the door open, paused, then stepped out. "Anybody there?"

Silence.

"Must have been the wind," said Sadie nervously.

Clarice examined the coffee can. "There's a message." She unfolded the notepaper. "*Marmalade is missing*," she read aloud. "*Come at once. Miss Parsnip, Crawley Mill."*

"Crawley Mill," groaned Sadie. "Nobody ever goes near Crawley Mill. Miss Parsnip is a witch, everyone knows that."

"Witch!" snorted Clarice scornfully. "Miss Parsnip is a retired metermaid. You read too much, Sadie. Grab your notebook and let's go."

"Now? In the dark?" protested Sadie.

"Our First Case," said Clarice disgustedly, "and all you can think about is darkness and witches!"

"Answer me this then," retorted Sadie. "If it was Miss Parsnip who left the message in our mailbox, why didn't she come in? She must have known we were in here. You know what I think? I think someone is trying to scare us; someone is playing a practical joke."

Clarice wrinkled her brow in thought. "We'll find out when we get over there. Let's go."

"Right, Chief," said Brick.

"Wait," said Sadie. "Before we all go rushing off we ought to discuss what the note means. 'Marmalade missing' sounds like someone broke into her preserves cupboard and stole the marmalade. Marmalade! I ask you, does that make sense?"

Clarice shot a look at Brick. "What do you think?"

Brick shrugged. "Don't see why not. Marmalade's great, especially on toast." He scratched his spiky head. "I like strawberry jam best though," he decided.

"Do you fall off that bike of yours a lot?" asked Sadie. "Maybe you ought to wear protective headgear. You're losing too much of that strawberry jam you use for brains."

"At least I'm not scared of witches," Brick countered after considering Sadie's suggestion for a few seconds.

"If a witch turned you into a frog it would be a total improvement," said Sadie.

"If you weren't so small I'd punch you out," said Brick quietly.

"Ribbit-ribbit," croaked Sadie.

"Cut it out!" yelled Clarice. "C'mon, let's get to work."

Ten minutes later the three detectives stood at the river bank, looking up at the dark shape of Crawley Mill with its huge waterwheel silhouetted against an almost-full moon.

Sadie pointed. "See! Bats flying out of the roof!"

"Bats are harmless," said Clarice uncertainly, "aren't they?"

"Harmless!" said Sadie scornfully. "Vampire bats suck your blood, everyone knows that! And everyone knows that witches live with bats in windmills and watermills. And tomorrow is Hallowe'en, when they all get together to perform dreadful witcheries. It's the scariest, spookiest night of the whole year! Those bats are probably carrying messages to other watermills and windmills all over the world. They're getting ready for tomorrow night. Harmless! Humph!"

The three sleuths stood watching the bats' silent flight across the face of the moon.

Sadie shivered. "Let's go home. I'm cold. This place gives me the creeps."

Clarice felt the same way, but she couldn't back down now. In as firm a voice as she could manage in the awesome silence of the night, she said, "We can't back out now. We have a Duty."

"Can't we rest first? My legs ache from all that bike-riding," said Sadie.

"Forward!" commanded Clarice, leading the way around the mill to the mill house. The house was attached to the mill and shared the same roof. But while over the mill it was full of holes, over the house the roof was intact. The three sleuths stumbled through the broken gate, along a gravel walk overgrown with grass and weeds, and up to the mill house door.

Clarice lifted the heavy iron knocker and let it fall with a resounding clang. The knocker bore the likeness of an animal. "Looks like a lion," said Clarice.

"It's a griffin," said Sadie. "It's got the head and wings of an eagle and the body of a lion. It's a mythical beast."

"You ought to be on Jeopardy," growled Brick.

They waited. There was no light at the door. Then the hall light came on and the door swung open on groaning hinges.

"Come in, dears," said Miss Parsnip, "I've been expecting you. Hot chocolate and butter-tarts await." Her voice crackled and creaked like crushed paper. Clarice had to admit to herself that Miss Parsnip sounded like a witch, and with her wrinkled face and sharp, pointed chin, she looked like one too.

Miss Parsnip turned and shuffled back inside. The three detectives paused, peering suspiciously into the interior of the old mill house.

But the light in the hallway glowed reassuringly bright and warm, and the furniture, though old, shone with friendly invitation. They entered and the door closed behind them with a quiet click.

Chapter 4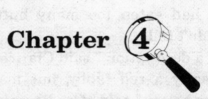

"Have some more, dears," said Miss Parsnip, passing the plate of butter tarts.

Three eager hands reached across the table. "These are great butter tarts," said Brick, starting on his fourth.

"Made from an ancient and secret recipe," said Miss Parsnip. "There is more hot chocolate in the jug and tea in the pot, help yourselves."

The three detectives had taken off their jackets and were gathered around a crackling fire in Miss Parsnip's big, old-fashioned kitchen.

When the tea and the hot chocolate and the butter tarts were all gone, Clarice got down to business. "Now then, Miss Parsnip, Sadie will take notes. She's the secretary."

"It's my cat," explained the old lady. "Her name is Marmalade."

"Cat? Did you say cat?" said Sadie.

"She has disappeared," said Miss Parsnip.

Brick gave a snort, whether in disgust or because he had eaten too many butter tarts Clarice couldn't tell.

"Give us a description," said Clarice.

"She's really a red tabby, but marmalade describes her better," said Miss Parsnip, "thick, chunky, orange marmalade." She thought for a few seconds. "Her eyes are green."

"Green you say," said Sadie with a note of hysteria in her voice, "you're sure about that? Must be an unusual colour for cats, green!"

Miss Parsnip didn't seem to notice Sadie's sarcasm.

"Long hair or short?" said Clarice.

"Quite long."

"Height?"

Miss Parsnip held a thin hand above the floor.

"Medium height," said Clarice. "Weight?"

"Well, I really don't . . . "

"A hundred and eighty kilos?" suggested

Sadie.

"Average weight," said Clarice shooting Sadie a dirty look.

"Yes, I'm sure you're right," agreed Miss Parsnip.

"Scars or marks?" said Clarice.

"Beg pardon?"

"Has Marmalade got any distinguishing scars or marks such as torn ears or a scarred nose?"

"Or tattoos?" said Sadie sweetly.

"Oh no, no scars, nothing of that sort. She's a very affectionate cat. She never goes after birds or mice or beetles, and only chases butterflies for the exercise. Marmalade is a lady."

Sadie appeared to be taking notes furiously, but in fact was drawing a madly-grinning cat chasing a butterfly.

"Collar?" said Clarice.

"Red, dear, red tabby . . ."

"I mean did she wear a collar?"

"Oh no, not her. Slipperier than Houdini she was when it came to collars."

"You got another cat called Houdini?" asked Brick.

"Houdini was a famous escape artist," said

Sadie scornfully. "He could get out of anything. One time, he escaped from —"

"When did Marmalade disappear?" interrupted Clarice.

"Today is Friday. She hasn't been home since dinner time Wednesday. That's two days exactly." She peered up at the tall and ancient grandfather clock in a corner of the cosy room. "She should have had her dinner an hour ago."

"Have you got a picture of Marmalade?" said Clarice.

The old lady rummaged through her papers on the sideboard and produced a colour snapshot. "This was taken in the summer," she said.

"Looks like a giant silkworm!" muttered Sadie.

"Do you have any reason to suspect Foul Play?" said Clarice.

"Yes, I do. She always comes home for her dinner." A tear started in the old lady's eye. "And she insists on Purrfect Catfood. . . . "

"The Purrfect food for purrfect cats," said Sadie who remembered TV jingles.

Miss Parsnip nodded her head. "She won't look at anything else." She pointed a bent finger at a shelf stacked high with identical blue cans of Purrfect Chopped Chicken. "She has never stayed away before. Poor Marmalade! I think she's been kidnapped."

"Catnapped," said Sadie.

"Snatched," said Brick.

"I rode my bicycle all the way to the police station this afternoon," said Miss Parsnip, "but Sergeant Teal told me they don't do cats. Only people." Tears filled her eyes. "I *must* find Marmalade soon, I *must!*"

"Don't worry, Miss Parsnip," said Clarice, "we'll find Marmalade for you. Leave it to us." She got up.

When they got outside, Clarice said to Sadie, "How could you think Miss Parsnip is a witch? Anyone can see what a nice old lady Miss Parsnip is. She made all that tea and hot chocolate for us, and those yummy butter tarts." She pushed off on her bicycle.

Sadie said, "Just because she acts like a nice old lady doesn't mean —"

"Besides," Clarice continued, ignoring her friend, "if she was a witch, she wouldn't need us to find her cat for her. If she was a witch, she could just cast a spell and Marmalade would magically appear. Trouble with you, Sadie, is you read too much. It's not good for you."

"Well, that's where you're wrong!" Sadie insisted. "That's where you're not using superior reasoning powers. The reason she needs us to help her find Marmalade is that with her *familiar* gone, her power is gone!"

"Her what?" said Clarice.

"Her familiar," explained Sadie patiently. "All witches have one. Usually a cat, but it could be a rabbit, or . . ."

"What does it do?"

"A witch gets her magic power through it from the spirits, and it helps her cast spells."

"You mean without her cat she can't work spells?" said Clarice, scoffing at her friend's seriousness.

"Only little spells," said Sadie, "like making those great butter tarts and sending that 'Help, I've lost my Marmalade' message into our mailbox. There was nobody outside the door when we opened it, remember?"

"Could have been left there earlier," said Clarice. "It was the wind that made the coffee can rattle."

"What wind? There was no wind. Besides, you checked the mailbox earlier, I saw you."

Clarice cycled a little faster, away from Sadie, and caught up to Brick. Sadie pedalled after her.

"Another thing, Clarice, why do you think Miss Parsnip said she *must* get Marmalade back soon? Why do you think she's in such a hurry, tell me that?"

Brick said, "Because she misses her cat?"

"No, birdbrain, it's because tomorrow is Hallowe'en!" said Sadie triumphantly. "Miss Parsnip *must* have her familiar for Hallowe'en or there'll be no Witches' Sabbath for her! She'll be like Wayne Gretzky without his hockey stick; like the Mona Lisa without her smile; she won't be able to work one single spell!"

Clarice gave Brick a look. He shrugged his shoulders at her.

Sadie said, "So don't believe me! What do I care!"

They cycled along in silence. Then Sadie said, "Missing cat!"

"What about it?" Clarice said.

"Well, it's a joke! Detective don't waste their time on missing cats. Finding cats isn't solving mysteries and fighting crime! Cats are for kids."

Clarice said, "Maybe you're right, Sadie, but it's a start. It'll help pay expenses. Besides, detectives *do* find missing people. And cats are just as important as people — so we can find missing cats."

Sadie reconsidered. "You're quite right, Clarice, cats *are* just as important as people. Maybe more important. I like cats better than most people I know." She glared at Brick. "But I never heard of a marmalade one before."

"She's an unusual colour, so she shouldn't be hard to find," Clarice said optimistically.

Brick said, "Marmalade."

They pushed up the Fairview slopes.

"Tomorrow's Saturday," said Clarice.

"Hallowe'en," said Sadie.

"We've got all day to find her," said Clarice.

"Marmalade," said Brick.

Chapter 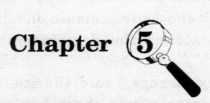 5

They met at the Agency office the next morning.

"I called Miss Parsnip," said Clarice. "Marmalade is still missing."

"Might be dead," said Sadie darkly, "killed by a rival witch."

"Cats got nine lives," said Brick.

"She's alive," said Clarice, "I know it."

"Your unerring sixth sense, no doubt," mumbled Sadie from the pages of her book.

Clarice ignored her friend's sarcasm. "Miss Parsnip said Marmalade is very affectionate. She's probably got a boyfriend somewhere. Cats can be very romantic. So let's move out. We start by searching the back alleys. On our bikes.

Quicker than walking. I've got a Hunch she's not very far away."

Two hours later the tired trio had covered most of the local territory without so much as a glimpse of a marmalade cat. They had seen a couple of black ones and a white one, and two black-and-white ones, and a couple of tabbies, even a sleek chocolate Siamese one, but nothing that matched the description of Marmalade.

"It's very strange," said Clarice. "Usually there are dozens of cats about, but we've seen very few."

"The explanation is simple," said Sadie. "It's Hallowe'en. Cats know it and they stay home. Only witches' cats come out after dark."

Clarice considered. Sadie was right about most things — except when she let her imagination run away with her. But you could tell it was Hallowe'en all right; as well as the grinning, leering pumpkin faces in everyone's windows and the cardboard monsters and witches on people's front doors, the day was cold and damp and gloomy with a light mist, which had made the search for Marmalade difficult. She shivered and pulled up the collar of her jacket.

"Let's quit," groaned Sadie. "I'm cold and I'm sick of searching for the stupid cat."

Clarice gasped. "Look, that's her — over there!" She pointed to a ginger-coloured giant of a cat that had leaped from nowhere on to a backyard wall not fifty paces from where they stood, and which now sat complacently licking its paws.

"That isn't Marmalade," said Sadie. "It's the wrong colour."

"Maybe not orange marmalade, but definitely lemon marmalade," said Clarice.

"And it's too big," said Sadie.

"No it's not, it's just about right if you take away some of that thick winter fur."

"What do you think, Brick?" said Sadie.

But Brick wasn't even listening; instead, he was balancing himself on his stationary bicycle, standing on the pedals in perfect equilibrium, like a swallow on a trembling branch.

"Well, I say it's Marmalade," said Clarice. "Let's go get her."

They leaned their bicycles against the wall and inched forward. "Quietly," said Clarice, "we don't want to frighten her off."

"Here, puss, puss," said Sadie in a sibilant whisper.

"Ma-*arm*-alade," cooed Clarice, walking tiptoe and wearing her friendliest and most fetching expression.

Quickly, lightly, Brick leaped up on to the wall. High above the girls, he stepped toward the cat, as lightly as a Russian ballet dancer on a stage.

The cat stopped licking his paw and regarded Brick with polite interest.

The girls stared at Brick in astonishment.

Brick flowed along the top of the wall, sat down easily beside the cat, and began to stroke its arching back as he whispered and gurgled at it. The cat seemed to understand him. It rubbed its head against the back of Brick's hand.

"Good work," Clarice called up to him. "Pass her down to us."

Brick picked up the big cat with one hand, leaned down and dropped it into Clarice's waiting arms. The animal might have been made of Silly Putty the way it moulded itself into whatever shape it was poured. It started to purr in Clarice's arms.

Brick jumped down off the wall and landed lightly on his feet.

"Well done, Baryshnikov," said Sadie.

"It's Brick," said Brick.

Sadie rolled her eyes and turned her attention to the cat. "She's cute," she said. "Let me hold her."

Clarice passed her over. "Yours is the only bike with a basket on the front, so you're in charge."

They started back for their bicycles.

"Told you it wouldn't be hard to find her," boasted Clarice. "It just takes Patience and Perseverance, that's all. Both are qualities a good Detective has got to develop. And Legwork. That's another important quality, Legwork is. It means you don't sit in your office waiting for Clues to walk in, you get out there and give it good old Legwork, good old Patience, and good old Perseverance."

"Hey, you! Where d'you think you're taking my cat?"

They spun around. A fat lady stood at the back gate with her arms folded across her chest.

Sadie walked back with the cat. "This is your cat?"

The woman's face was like granite. With her

eyes flashing, she reached out and tore the cat from Sadie's arms. "You kids these days are all the same. What d'you reckon on doing with a cat that don't belong to you? Robbers and thieves and cat molesters is what you are. What kinda parents've got such kids I don't know. Where'd you learn such stuff, eh?"

A man with a face like a walrus poked his head out from behind the woman's bulky arms. "What's the matter, Dolly? These kids botherin' you?"

"Call the police, Herbert, I've caught a buncha cat thieves."

The little man disappeared.

"Now look here," said Clarice, "you've got a nerve calling us all that stuff. You want to know what I think of you and your fat cat —?"

Sadie quickly cut Clarice off by pushing herself to the front and addressing the woman in a polite tone of voice. "Take no notice of my friend," she said, "we're on a case. We're searching for Miss Parsnip's marmalade cat. Your cat just happened to fit the —"

"*Marmalade* cat? Our Ginger is no ordinary marmalade cat!"

Sadie said, "We meant no harm to your cat. It was a mistake. We're sorry."

"Police is coming." Walrus-face was back, grinning from behind the woman's elbow. "We had Ginger more'n ten years. He's a Ginger Tabby, same as the one in the Ginger Tabby Commercial for Ginger Tabby Catfood. Had her ten years we have, right Dolly?"

"When are they coming, Herbert?" said Dolly. The cat had gone to sleep under the roof of her ample bosom.

"Any minute now," said Herbert, peering around over his narrow shoulders.

"Ginger's got personality," said Dolly with a sniff. "There's lots would like to get their hands on Ginger, you bet! Cats with personality earns millions in movies and TV. But our Ginger's not for sale at any price."

"Here they come," said Herbert.

A police patrol cruiser pulled into the back lane and stopped beside the small group. Two officers stepped out of the car. "Are you Mrs. Varden?" said the one with the moustache.

"That's right," said Dolly. She delivered her cat-thief speech again while Herbert grinned and nodded his head and Clarice's face grew redder and redder to match her hair until she finally exploded. "She's full of baloney! The old —"

Sadie cut in again. "It's all a mistake, officer. We are three private investigators trying to trace a missing cat."

"May I see your ID?" said the officer.

"ID?" Clarice raised her titian eybrows. "We don't have ID."

The officer smiled, and winked at his partner. "Private investigators are required to carry ID cards. In the meantime I'm going to have to ask you to stop seizing people's cats without a proper search and seize warrant, OK?"

"OK, officer," said Sadie.

"Quite right," said Dolly. "Cats aren't for seizing by anybody. Cats are private property."

Later, riding home, Sadie said, "Told you so. Told you it wasn't Marmalade. Your trouble, Clarice, is you go around seizing things without listening to reason. And what happened to this wonderful sixth sense of yours? It doesn't apply to cats, obviously."

Clarice gave her friend a dark look. "Well, I don't see how these so-called superior reasoning powers of yours are helping much either." She pedalled in silence. Then she said, "Anyone could make a mistake over a cat. One cat is very much like another. It wasn't our fault."

"We should have brought Miss Parsnip's picture of Marmalade," said Sadie.

"You're right," admitted Clarice, and pedalled faster to catch up to Brick.

Chapter  6

When they got back to headquarters they were tired and hungry.

"I'm tired," said Sadie.

"I'm hungry," said Brick.

Clarice said, "I'll go raid the refrigerator. Wait here."

Five minutes later she was back carrying a bulging brown bag. "Help yourselves. I got some leftover tuna casserole . . ."

"Ugh!" said Sadie.

" . . . and half a pizza, and some apple pie, and a bag of chocolate chip cookies . . ."

"Yum," said Brick.

" . . . and I brought a calligraphy pen and

scissors and some old Christmas cards for you to cut up, Sadie."

"I'm not *that* hungry!"

"Don't be dumb. I want you to make ID cards for all of us. All Detectives have ID cards. Not having ID cards was downright embarrassing."

"Can't it wait?" said Sadie, who was about to bite into a cookie.

"No," said Clarice. "Write O'Brien Detective Agency on the top and our names underneath, and leave a space for me to sign."

Sadie put down her cookie reluctantly, sat down at the desk and started to cut out three ID cards. Then she pushed her tongue out the side of her mouth as she concentrated on the writing. Sadie was a perfectionist. Whenever she did something she had to get it right or she was not satisfied. When she came to Brick's card, she said, "I don't even know his last name."

Brick, his mouth full, said nothing.

Sadie said, "Brick, what's your last name?"

Silence. It was as if he hadn't heard her.

"Just write Brick," said Clarice.

When Sadie had finished, Clarice inspected them. "Good work." She signed them 'Clarice O'Brien' with little circles over the i's. "Carry them at all times. Now, when you two have finished feeding your faces we'll go search for Marmalade again."

"But it's Hallowe'en!" said Sadie.

"So what?" said Clarice.

"What do you mean 'so what'? It's trick-or-treat. We can't go searching for Marmalade and miss all those treats!"

"Trick-or-treat is for kids," said Clarice, "not Detectives. But you go ahead. We'll manage without you, right Brick?"

"Right, Chief," said Brick.

"Duty comes first," said Clarice. "We've been handed a Job and we gotta do it. Responsibility. We gotta find that cat, Hallowe'en or no Hallowe'en."

"I don't want to go home," Sadie grumbled, "but I'm sick of searching for that dumb cat. It's no fun. If we can't go trick-or-treating we should at least be solving a real crime."

"If we can't solve a simple cat disappearance," Clarice argued, "how can we expect to solve something complicated like a robbery for instance? Answer me that!"

"It's boring," said Sadie. "Gargling would be more exciting."

Brick threw himself onto his sack of potatoes. Clarice started pacing up and down and tapping her teeth with the rubber tip of a pencil. "We need a Brainwashing Session," she said thoughtfully.

"Brainstorming," Sadie corrected her.

"Let us examine the Facts," said Clarice. "First, Miss Parsnip's cat goes missing for no reason."

Brick sat up. His amber eyes glowed. "Missing from home," he said.

"Second, although Foul Play is suspected by owner, owner offers no supporting evidence of Foul Play."

"You mean the cat wasn't snatched, Chief?" said Brick.

"Probably not." Clarice tapped her lower lip with the rubber-tipped pencil. "Who would want to catnap a kid — I mean kidnap a cat — I ask you! The only explanation Miss Parsnip offers is that Marmalade has never stayed away before. Well, cats go missing all the time. If they didn't, there'd never be any stray cats. And everyone knows that there *are* stray cats — a neighbourhood just wouldn't be a neighbourhood without a few stray cats — therefore, it stands to reason that Marmalade has probably strayed and is not the victim of Foul Play."

Brick frowned as he tried to follow Clarice's relentless logic. In the end he gave up. "Wow!" he said.

"Third, Marmalade is an affectionate cat. She has never disappeared before . . ."

"This is like a bedtime story," said Sadie in her best sarcastic manner. "I can hardly wait to hear how it all turns out."

Clarice continued her pacing and tapping. There was silence in the garden shed.

"Marmalade is fed Purrfect Catfood every day," said Clarice.

"Chopped chicken," said Sadie.

Clarice said, "You'd think a cat might get tired of the same thing every day."

Brick said, "Miss Parsnip said she likes it the best."

"I like pineapple pizza," said Clarice, "but not every day. I'd go ape if I had to eat pineapple pizza every day for the rest of my life."

Sadie pulled off her glasses and started to clean the lenses with a special tiny square of cloth she carried for the purpose. She gave a long sigh of boredom.

"I've got a Hunch!" said Clarice.

Sadie groaned.

"What is it, Chief?" said Brick.

"Marmalade is at Granville Market!"

"Your last hunch was a major disaster," Sadie reminded her friend.

Clarice ignored her. "For the last few days the wind has been coming up the inlet from Burrard Bridge and past Granville Market. You can smell the sea. And something else."

"Is all this leading to something?" Sadie smiled sweetly which meant she felt another sarcastic comment coming on.

"You can smell raw fish and shrimp!" said Clarice confidently. "My Powerful Sixth Sense tells me that Marmalade followed her nose to Granville Market. Cats love fish. Especially when they've been fed canned food day after day, and *especially* when that canned cat food is always the same flavour day after day."

"Chopped chicken," said Brick thoughtfully.

"I hate fish," said Sadie.

Clarice and Brick ignored her.

"Well?" Clarice said to Brick. "What do you think?"

"I think you got something, Chief," said Brick.

"Good grief!" said Sadie. "What's all this 'Chief' stuff?"

"He's right," said Clarice. "I'm the Chief Detective, so Chief is what I get called from now on."

Sadie's eyes glinted behind her spectacles. "What do I get called?"

"Brick is Number Two. You're Number Three."

"But that's not fair. I joined before him. I should be Number Two."

"You're a year younger than us," said Clarice. "Besides, you're the secretary. You're not promoted to Detective yet. Brick was taken on as a detective, remember?"

Sadie scowled. "That's not fair." She kicked Brick's potato sack. "I'm your best friend, Clarice, so I'm Number Two." She turned to Brick. "You'll have to be happy as Number Three, Wonderboy."

Brick shrugged. He didn't seem to care.

Clarice sighed. "Oh, all right, have it your way, Sadie, but you're still Secretary."

Sadie grinned.

"So what do you think of my Hunch, Number Two?"

"Call it a hunch if you like," said Sadie, "but

it seems to me you *reasoned* this one out for a change." She jammed her book into her jacket pocket. "Let's give it a try, Clarice."

"You gotta call me Chief from now on," said Clarice. "Ready to move out?"

"Yes, Clarice," said Sadie sweetly.

Brick slid off his potato sack. "Ready, Chief!" He dropped into a crouch. "Aiee!" he cried, slashing at the air around an innocent garden rake which was standing in a corner of the shed minding its own business.

Sadie rolled her eyes.

"Granville Market, here we come," said Clarice.

Chapter 7

Granville Market was busy. The three detectives searched around the fish dock and the garbage bins along the waterfront. "Marmalade," they called, but there came no answering meows. Then they searched around the huge market building, and poked around the wharves and the hotels and the restaurants. Marmalade didn't answer their calls.

By late afternoon the fog had disappeared and a pale egg-yolk sun was attempting to brighten up what was left of the day.

"I'm hungry," announced Brick.

"My feet hurt," moaned Sadie.

They trooped into the market. Clarice bought

some peanut brittle, Sadie bought a bag of mixed nuts and raisins, and Brick bought an orange and some beef jerky. Then they went outside again and leaned over the guardrail behind the market. They chewed in silence, watching a sleek motor yacht leave the harbour and head out under Burrard Bridge for the open sea. Over on the far shore, the mountains were partly hidden in cloud.

Brick hurled his orange peel at the pigeons with little cries of destruction. Clarice and Sadie chewed silently. Brick aimed the last of his orange peel at a pair of bored seagulls perched up on the guardrail near the Arts Club wharf. "Aieee, aieee!" he cried. The seagulls shot him a look of disgust and flew off to the pilings near the Aquabus ferry dock where it was more peaceful.

"Better head home," said Clarice despondently.

"Wait," said Sadie.

"What is it, Number Two?"

"I hear a cat crying," said Sadie.

"Where?"

"It's coming from over there." Sadie pointed at the roof of the Arts Club.

"You hear anything, Number Three?" said Clarice.

"No, Chief."

"Come on, let's take a look," said Clarice.

Sadie led the way eagerly.

"Hear anything?" said Clarice.

Sadie shook her head. "It's stopped."

They waited.

"There it is again!" said Sadie. "It's up on the roof." She stepped back and craned her neck. "There she is!" she yelled.

Sadie was right. High up on the corrugated metal roof an orange cat sat, crying down at them.

Clarice examined Miss Parsnip's snapshot. "That's her!"

"Marmalade!" yelled Sadie.

The cat cried louder.

"Must be her," said Clarice. "Why doesn't she climb down?"

"Tin roof's too slippery," Sadie guessed. "And with that overhang it'd be like climbing down off the top of a greasy mushroom."

"How will we get her down?" said Clarice.

"Leave it to me, Chief," said Brick. He began climbing up the drainpipe. He was like a cat himself, a thin cat with spiky yellow hair. The two girls were astonished by his speed and confidence.

"Be careful, Number Three," Clarice called, "that roof is dangerous!" They watched as Brick moved surely up the pipe and rolled himself gracefully onto the roof. He crawled toward the cat.

The cat watched him. It had stopped crying, and was now huddled against the ledge of a dormer window which was set into the roof. The roof was tin and sloping and treacherous.

"If Number Three slips," said Clarice, "he'll slide right down off the roof and break his neck."

"No need to worry," said Sadie, "he won't get hurt; he weighs less than a Canada goose."

Brick poured toward the cat like pancake syrup, slow and smooth and silent. When he was within a few feet of the cowering cat he made a noise: "Hrrrrrmmmmmnngg."

"You hear that?" said Clarice.

"I hear it," said Sadie.

"He's the Cat Man," said Clarice.

Marmalade padded over to Brick and rubbed her arching back on his faded jeans. Brick picked her up and, holding her to his thin chest, began a slow slide down the roof, sneakers flat in front of him to control his rate of descent.

"Like a human fly," said Clarice.

Brick reached the lower edge of the roof, swivelled his invisible hips around the drainpipe and slid easily to the ground.

Just as Clarice and Sadie started toward Brick and Marmalade, a collection of creatures, quaint and small, came screaming along the alleyway between the market and the Arts Club. They were tiny Hallowe'en children dressed as goblins, ghosts and trolls.

The cat, terrified by the noise, leaped out of Brick's arms and fled down the alley.

Chapter  8

The cat streaked past the Arts Club and out onto Johnston Street.

"After her!" yelled Clarice as they charged out into the one-way street. "Stop that cat!"

The children in the Hallowe'en outfits heard the cry. They were closer to Marmalade than the three sleuths. They swerved, screaming, after the terrified cat — right into the path of an oncoming car.

When the driver of the small red car saw three wild goblins, three ghosts with white faces, two green trolls, and three children coming at him he slammed on his brakes. And was struck in the rear by a delivery van: crash! The delivery van was sandwiched by a black sedan: crunch!

Meanwhile, the detectives followed Marmalade and the eight small creatures down Tower Mast Road and into a shop called Lobster Man. When they got inside they saw the trick-or-treaters hanging over the edges of two bubbling water tanks full of live lobsters. There was no sign of Marmalade, and the costumed children did not know where the cat had gone.

"Search underneath the tanks," yelled Clarice. The detectives crawled around on their hands and knees until they were sore. No Marmalade. They stood up and leaned against one of the tanks. The water in the tank bubbled fiercely.

"Lobsters are ugly," said Sadie, peering into the tank.

"Some people are uglier," said Brick. He leaned his yellow head over the rim of the tank and began to make a sound: "Klikkgglikkgg." The lobsters started to become excited. The Hallowe'en trolls and ghosts and goblins imitated Brick's clicking. The lobsters became more excited.

Clarice said, "Never mind the lobsters. Search for the cat!"

Brick's strange clicking sounds and those of

the goblins and ghosts were beginning to cause such agitation in the tanks that the water swelled over the sides and slopped onto the floor.

Clarice said, "Number Two, stop him!"

"Get out of here!" came a loud voice.

It was the lobster man himself, charging down on Brick and his goblin helpers. His face was boiling red with rage and his huge arms waved about over his head like pincers. "Get out!" he screamed.

Marmalade, frightened by the sudden noise, shot out from her hiding place under the counter into the lobster man's charging feet. The lobster man pitched forward with a loud cry and fell headfirst into the closest tank. The tank toppled over and fell with a mighty crash into the one beside it. The two tanks spilled their lobsters out in a sudden wave of water, and a river of crustaceans flowed out the door, down the sidewalk, and into the deep waters of Broker's Bay.

It had all happened so fast that the three detectives and the Hallowe'en goblins could only stand and stare in horror as the liberated creatures spilled happily into the sea.

Clarice was the first to recover. Waving her arms frantically in the direction of Duranleau

Street she yelled, "Marmalade! Quick! After her!"

The trick-or-treaters disappeared quickly out the door in the opposite direction: they had had enough.

"Come back here!" yelled the lobster man who was still trying to stagger to his feet. But the three sleuths had taken off after the cat.

They galloped madly down the street, slid around the corner at Blackberry's book store, skimmed past the arts and crafts shop, and plunged into the market.

"There she goes!" cried Sadie.

They hurled themselves along past the flower shop and the ice cream shop and the Belgian chocolate shop and the bakery, and just as they reached the stalls of fruit and vegetables, Marmalade twisted sharply under one stall and out another. A tall thin lady shrieked with fright when she spied the streak of marmalade fur, and threw her loaded carrier bags into the air. The bags fell onto the head of a well-dressed, haughty man who gave a curse and fell sideways into the oranges. The stall came crashing down like a domino onto the next stall, scattering apples and grapefruits and pumpkins all over the floor.

Screaming shoppers slipped on the rolling fruit. The air was blue with language unsuitable for the tender ears of children. But instead of covering their ears, the three cat-chasers crawled about on their hands and knees amidst the confusion, searching for Marmalade.

"You see her?" yelled Clarice.

"No, Chief," said Brick.

The cat was nowhere to be seen.

"Disappeared," said Sadie helplessly, "completely disappeared!"

Chapter 9

"So now what?" complained Sadie a few minutes later.

"We split up," said Clarice. "The market closes soon. Meet here at the Fudge Shop in ten minutes." She reached up over her head and helped herself to her fourth free sample of chocolate ripple fudge. They were all chewing rapidly. "And if you see Marmalade don't frighten her off, just tell us where and we'll all go along and help catch her." They each helped themselves to another piece of fudge. "Keep your eyes open," ordered Clarice as they separated.

When she saw them coming back ten minutes later, the Fudge Shop lady removed her plates of samples from the counter and began closing her shop.

"Any luck, Number Two?" asked Clarice.

Sadie shook her head. "Clarice, could we go home now? I'm getting a headache from this boring case."

"Number Three?"

"No, Chief." Brick looked alert and poised.

"She's hiding *somewhere*," said Clarice. "We'll have to wait until everyone has gone home. Then we'll find her. The market will be empty and quiet."

"But how can we do that?" said Sadie.

"I have a Plan," said Clarice.

Sadie groaned.

"What kind of plan, Chief?" said Brick.

"Like Marmalade, we hide. The market is closing. When it's closed, we creep from our hiding places and find her. Simple. The best Plan is always the simplest Plan, right?"

"Right, Chief."

"Right, Chief," mimicked Sadie.

"Cut it out, Number Two."

Sadie scowled. "And where do you think we can hide where we won't be discovered and arrested?"

"The washrooms," said Clarice.

Sadie groaned again.

"Are you with me?" said Clarice.

"You can count on me, Chief."

"Number Two?"

"I don't like it, Clarice."

"Chief," said Clarice.

Sadie mumbled something, but it didn't sound like "Chief."

The two washrooms were side by side around the corner from the Fudge Shop.

"Meet here in half an hour," Clarice said to Brick as the two girls pushed their way into the women's washroom.

The washroom was empty. The two girls entered separate cubicles and sat down to wait.

"Clarice, this is stupid," said Sadie to her wall.

"You're supposed to call me Chief, not Clarice," Clarice said to her wall.

"What if someone finds us here?"

"They won't."

"But, Clarice, what if they do?"

"All they can do is ask us to leave."

They sat in silence for a minute. Then Sadie gave a big sigh. "What if we can't get out of the market? What if we're locked in all night?"

"Stop worrying, Number Two. We'll get out."

"Clarice, I wish you wouldn't keep calling me Number Two; it's depressing to be a number. I hate it."

"It's only when we're on a Case."

"Seems to me we're always on a case lately. Life has become a permanent case. I liked you much better, Clarice, before you decided to be a detective. We used to trick-or-treat together, remember?"

"Sadie, if someone comes in, lift your feet off the floor. That way they'll think the place is empty."

"You called me Sadie."

"No I didn't."

"Yes you did, I heard you. You said, 'Sadie, if someone comes in, take your feet off the floor.'"

"Didn't."

"Did so."

Silence.

"I can see your feet from here, Clarice. Are those the sneakers you got last summer?"

"Stop calling me Clarice."

" 'Cause if they are, you need new ones already. The pink and blue is all faded and dirty and they don't look so nice any more. Look at mine." Sadie pushed her feet nearer to the gap under the partition. "I got these the same time as you, and they're still good. But mine are Bobcats, not imitations. Maybe that's what makes the difference."

Clarice said nothing.

"Yours have plastic on the toes, mine have rubber."

Silence.

"Rubber is natural, plastic isn't. Did you know plastic is made from oil, Clarice? That it's polluting our planet?"

Silence.

"Oil on the beaches, oil in the atmosphere, oil everywhere. Kills all the seabirds and . . . Clarice, are you there?"

Silence.

"Clarice?"

"*Chief!*" said Clarice through clenched teeth.

"That's mainly why I don't like cheap sneakers. I care too much about our planet, Clarice, to buy plastic sneakers. Don't you care about our planet, Clarice?"

Silence.

"That Brick is really weird. Look at how he talks to animals. And the way he looks at you with those eyes. And you know what?"

"What?"

"I don't think his elevator goes all the way up to the top floor."

"Huh?"

"The lights are on but there's nobody home?"

"*Sadie* . . . !"

"His brains. I don't think he's got very many."

"I like Number Three," said Clarice. "Maybe he's not too smart, but he doesn't put on airs or make sarcastic remarks like some people. And you can depend on him."

There was a long silence.

"Clarice?"

Silence.

"Clarice, are you there? I can't see your feet."

"Let's move out," said Clarice. She opened the cubicle door and switched off the washroom light.

"Clarice, don't leave me in the dark, wait!" wailed Sadie.

They slipped out the door and stood close together, eyes and ears alert. The market was dim and deserted.

And strangely quiet.

"I've never seen it like this," whispered Sadie, "it's spooky." She held tightly to Clarice's arm.

Clarice rapped lightly on the men's wash-room door. The door was jerked open. Brick's slight figure was framed in the doorway. "Switch off the light, Number Three!" said Clarice in a fierce whisper.

"Sorry, Chief." Brick switched off the light.

"C'mon," said Clarice firmly, "let's go find that crazy cat."

Chapter 10

They crept along the dark aisles full of fruit and vegetables. Dim lights had been left on over a few of the stalls, and they threw eerie shadows across the draped and covered stalls and along the aisles.

"Careful," whispered Clarice, "there might be someone still here."

"My superior hearing ability tells me that everyone has gone home," said Sadie.

"Does your superior hearing ability tell you where Marmalade is?" said Clarice.

"Wait up," said Sadie, "let me listen properly." She stood with an ear raised toward the market ceiling.

"I don't hear nothing," said Brick.

"Don't hear *anything*," said Sadie.

"Me neither," said Clarice, "so let's keep moving."

They padded silently along the dark aisles until they came to a shop called The Stockmarket which sold soup. They stopped. Clarice said, "You hear anything, Number Two?"

Sadie listened. "Only the traffic on Granville Bridge, that's all."

"Humph!" said Clarice.

Sadie said, "What about your so-called sixth sense, Clarice? Shouldn't you be having one of your hunches about now?"

Clarice ignored Sadie's sarcasm. "You hear anything, Number Three?"

"No, Chief."

"Wait!" said Sadie. "I think I can hear something."

They listened.

"What?" said Clarice.

"Something," said Sadie. "Along that aisle." She pointed, and started walking on tiptoe. The others followed.

At the end of the aisle they came to a shop called Longliner, which sold fish.

Clarice said, "Hear anything?"

"No," said Sadie.

"Maybe she's in the fish shop looking for scraps," said Clarice, "but we can't get in with that steel grille all the way around the front of the shop."

"Should I try calling her?" said Brick.

"Worth a try," said Clarice.

"She's in there!" said Sadie. "I can hear something moving."

Brick said, "Hrrrrrmmmmmnngg."

Silence. They waited.

"Can you still hear her, Number Two?"

"I can hear her listening to us," said Sadie.

Clarice said, "Can you really talk to animals, Number Three?"

"Most animals," Brick nodded.

"Try again."

"Hrrrrrmmmmmnngg," said Brick.

"I don't believe you really *talk* to them," said Sadie, "not in their own language."

Brick appeared to be considering this idea. He frowned and blinked. Then he said, "People talk to their cats and dogs. They do it all the time."

"Yes," said Sadie, "but that's human talk, not animal talk."

Brick scratched his head. "People could learn animal talk if they wanted to."

"How?" said Clarice.

Brick shrugged his thin shoulders and thought for a while. "By listening real careful to what animals say," he replied.

Sadie snorted.

Brick said, "Hrrrrrmmmmnngg," into the shop.

"Well, I believe him," said Clarice. "Where did you learn all this, Number Three?"

"My parents are English," he said slowly as if he had trouble remembering who his parents were, "but I was born in Ngamba in editorial Africa . . ."

"*Equatorial* Africa, you mean," said Sadie in her know-it-all voice, "not editorial."

"Go on," said Clarice.

"It means the hottest part," explained Sadie. "Not you, Number Two, be quiet!"

" . . . and when I was a baby," continued Brick, "I crawled out of my crib . . ."

"Out of your mind," muttered Sadie.

" . . . and got lost in the jungle. I was raised by a family of lions . . ."

"Lions?" said Clarice.

"Lions!" exclaimed Sadie.

" . . . My father found me eventually, when I was five." Brick stopped to gather his thoughts. "By then I'd learned to live in the jungle and talk animal talk."

It was Brick's longest speech yet. The girls stared at him, astonished for the third time that day. Even Sadie was silent for a moment. When she managed to get her brain connected to her tongue again, she said, "Or maybe what *really* happened was you got hit over the head with a bundle of 'Tarzan of the Apes' comics."

But Brick ignored her. "Hrrrrrmmmmnngg," he murmured into the steel grille of the fish shop.

"I hear a cat purr," said Sadie.

"That's Number Three," said Clarice.

"No, I mean from inside the shop."

"Hrrrrrmmmmnngg," whispered Brick softly.

And out stepped Marmalade, squeezing herself through the grille. She made straight for Brick and rubbed her back against his legs. Brick stooped and scooped her up. "Hrrrrrmmmmnngg," he said into one marmalade ear. The cat purred and settled herself contentedly into Brick's arms.

The two girls gathered around. "So cute," said Sadie, stroking the cat's thick orange fur with her fingers.

"Thanks," said Brick.

"Not you, Doctor Doolittle," said Sadie sourly.

"Good work, Number Three," said Clarice.

"Thanks, Chief."

"What about me?" said Sadie. "It was I who led —"

"Good work, Number Two," said Clarice.

"Thank you," said Sadie.

"Let's get out of here," said Clarice. "Follow me."

They made for the exit. Clarice tried the door. It opened. "It's the kind that locks from the outside," she said with a sigh of relief.

Outside, it was dark. Granville Island was deserted. The shops had all closed, and the theatres and restaurants were not yet busy. The costumed children had disappeared, gone to collect their treats. The sky had cleared enough for the moon to show its three-quarter face. A breeze was getting up. A forest of bobbing sailboat masts stood dark against the open arc of Burrard Bridge.

Clarice zipped up her worn ski jacket. Sadie pulled up the collar of her fleece-lined designer denim jacket. Brick curled the marmalade fur into his thin chest.

"Let's wrap the Case up," said Clarice, "and get this runaway cat home."

The cat, happy to be rescued, wore an expression of feline relief on her handsome marmalade face.

Chapter 11

Marmalade rode happily in the wire basket on the front of Sadie's bicycle. She was going home.

The three detectives sped quickly down the moonlit streets of Fairview Slopes and through the Hallowe'en night. From every window, porch, and balcony pumpkin faces, glowing orange with flickering candles, leered menacingly into the darkness. Skeletons and bats and monsters lurked everywhere to terrify even the bravest hearts.

"Trick or treat!" cried the tiny elves and hobbits. Ghosts and goblins haunted the hedgerows; witches and warlocks prowled the porches. "Trick or treat!" chanted the trolls and gnomes.

"Trick or treat!" rumbled the robots and spacemen.

Sadie, as she sped along behind Clarice and Brick, looked longingly at the Hallowe'en creatures trooping from door to door, and yearned to be one of them, carrying her heavy bag of candies and chocolate and who knew what other goodies.

But it was not to be. Ten minutes later they had left the busy streets behind and were standing outside Miss Parsnip's door at Crawley Mill.

Brick knocked. They waited. It was very quiet.

Sadie pointed to a broom which was leaning up against the side of the house a few metres away from where they stood. "See!" she whispered hoarsely. "Miss Parsnip's broom. Most witches fly on a broom. Basic witch transportation, everyone knows that. She's got it parked out here ready for her trip."

Clarice sighed. Brick growled.

"Knock again," said Clarice.

Brick let the heavy, lion-eagle knocker fall twice. The sounds punctuated the silence of the night like cannon shots. The three sleuths stood back from the door, waiting.

The moon wrapped its cold light around the

old mill. The hoot of an owl came up from the woods.

Sadie shivered. "Spooky!"

"Who's there?" came Miss Parsnip's crackly voice from the other side of the door. She sounded quite upset.

"It's only us, Miss Parsnip," said Clarice. "We found Marmalade."

The door swung quickly open with a creak and a groan. Miss Parsnip stood wide-eyed, her hands at her mouth. "Marmalade!" she cried. Her eyes grew rounder. "You found her! My own Marmalade!" She gave a sob.

Brick dropped the cat into Miss Parsnip's welcoming arms. She clasped the happy cat to her bony chest. "Come in, come in," she croaked.

"I'll wait here," said Sadie.

Miss Parsnip said, "It's warmer and cosier inside." She turned and led the way. She was wearing a long black coat that brushed the floor as she walked. Brick followed her in. Sadie didn't move.

"Come on, Number Two," said Clarice, waiting for her.

"I'd sooner wait here," said Sadie, her voice small in the quiet of the night.

Clarice put her arm around her friend's shoulders. "It's too cold out here, Sadie. Come on. Maybe there'll be butter tarts." She led Sadie into Miss Parsnip's tiny living room.

"I cannot ask you all to stay for tea," said Miss Parsnip. "I must rush away." She hurried over to the window, Marmalade still in her arms, and parted the curtain to peer outside. She gave a cackle full of delight. "Gibbous moon on Hallowe'en, fairest sight you've ever seen!"

The threesome stood in the middle of the room watching her.

"Excuse me, children, while I take care of my milkmouth Marmalade." She rushed into the kitchen where she could be heard clattering and chattering and pouring a bowl of milk for Marmalade.

"What's a gibbous moon?" whispered Clarice.

"Moon almost full," said Sadie. "Listen!"

They listened, but all Clarice could hear was Miss Parsnip's sing-song cackle in the other room. "What's she saying?"

"Hush," said Sadie, her ear turned toward the kitchen. Then she turned to Clarice. "She's chanting to herself, just like a witch."

"What is she chanting?" asked Clarice.

Sadie said, " 'Marmalade sleek, Marmalade fat, welcome home my wandering cat. Cellar black and dungeon deep, cannot from thy mistress keep.' "

Clarice scratched her titian head.

"Witches talk in rhyme all the time," said Sadie.

Miss Parsnip reappeared. She was opening her purse. "How can I ever thank you, dears? How much is your fee for finding my precious Marmalade?" The purse was big and black and heavy.

"The flat rate for a Cat Case," said Clarice, "is ten dollars. And if you want to take our advice, Miss Parsnip, you shouldn't feed your cat the same Purrfect Chopped Chicken every day."

"But she loves Purrfect Chopped Chicken," said Miss Parsnip.

"Not every day, she doesn't," said Brick. "Animals are the same as people."

Miss Parsnip reached down into the bottom of her purse, almost to her elbow, and found a handful of bills which she pressed into Clarice's hands.

Clarice stared at the money. "But we can't take all this," she protested, "it's too much!"

Miss Parsnip slung her purse over her shoulder and began fumbling in her closet. "You earned it, dears." She pulled out a wide black hat and jammed it on her head. "Marmalade is worth more to me than gold. She was lost but now she's found."

Marmalade padded back into the room licking her whiskers with her tiny pink tongue. Miss Parsnip bent down, swept her up, and thrust her into the big black purse.

"And now I must go, dears. I'm very late. Let yourselves out. And come again for tea and butter tarts. Pull the door closed as you leave. Goodbye!"

And she was gone, rushing out the door, her black coat flapping around her ankles and Marmalade's happy head sticking up out of her black purse.

The three catfinders stared at one another in astonishment. Then Clarice said, "Come on." She stuffed the money into her jacket pocket and led the way out of the house. Brick pulled the door closed behind them.

There was no sign of Miss Parsnip.

"Which way did she go?" said Clarice, peering along the empty moonlit road in bewilderment.

"Look," said Sadie pointing to the wall of the

house, "the broomstick!"

Clarice and Brick stared.

"It's gone!" said Sadie.

* * *

"Stands to reason," said Sadie, "once Miss Parsnip gets her familiar back again, she's able to cast spells and fly her broomstick and perform all her witcheries. Seems perfectly obvious to me, at least."

They were riding their bicycles slowly home along River Road.

Clarice said, "Half of the money goes into the Agency for future expenses, and the other half we split for ourselves."

"For chocolate ripple fudge," said Brick.

"So go ahead, don't believe me," said Sadie.

"Look, Number Two," said Clarice, "maybe you're right about Miss Parsnip being a witch, I don't know. But we solved the Case — the Case is closed, that's all that matters. Miss Parsnip could be Cleopatra for all I care. If Cleopatra hired us to find her lost snake and we found it, then that would be the end of it!"

They rode along in silence for a while.

"We solved our First Case," said Clarice. "It took Patience and it took Guts and we did it. Being Secretary, Number Two, it's part of your job to make sure the money is safe in the Agency account. You could keep it in one of those clay pots in the shed — I mean the Office — and hide it with all the other clay pots up on the top shelf."

Sadie didn't answer. She was deep in thought.

"Number Two?" said Clarice.

"What?"

"What do you think?"

"I still think Miss Parsnip is a witch. She looks like a witch, she dresses like a witch, and she talks like a witch."

"You haven't been listening."

"You've got a nerve, Clarice — "

"*Chief*," corrected Clarice firmly.

"*Clarice!*" said Sadie. " — saying I'm not listening! Whose Superior Hearing found Marmalade? Come on, tell me! Whose? Answer me!"

Clarice noticed that her friend was starting to talk in capitals. "You did a great job, Number Two. We wouldn't have found the cat without you. But don't forget it was my Powerful Sixth Sense that led us to Granville Market in the first place, and without Number Three we could never have caught Marmalade. We're a Team!"

"Team," Brick repeated, nodding his head in agreement.

"Hmph!" said Sadie.

"When do we start on the Cleopatra case, Chief?" said Brick.

"The what case?" said Clarice.

"The kid who lost her snake," said Brick.

Sadie rolled her eyes. "And I suppose you speak snake language too!"

Brick grinned. "Well, I . . ."

"Cleopatra is not a kid," Clarice explained patiently, cutting in before Sadie started a fight, "she was an Arabian queen who lived thousands of years ago."

"Egyptian," Sadie corrected, "not Arabian."

They cycled along in silence, Sadie again deep in thought.

Then Clarice said, "Number Two . . ."

"Huh?" said Sadie.

" . . . you're still Secretary, of course, but . . ."

"Yeah?"

" . . . you're also promoted to the full rank of Detective, same as me and Number Three."

"Gee!" Sadie's bespectacled and moonlit face shone with happiness. "Thanks, Chief!"

Chapter 12

On Monday, after school, Clarice and Sadie waited for Brick to arrive at the office. He was late.

Sadie untied her ribbon and began to comb out her long hair. "What we need in here is a mirror, not seed catalogues and empty coffee cans," she complained.

"If you can ever stop fussing with your hair there's a couple of messages for you to write down in your notebook. They were in the mailbox."

"Police shows on TV always have mirrors so officers can check their appearance. The very least we could have is a hand mirror."

At half-past four they heard someone outside. Clarice opened the door. But it wasn't Brick. It was a tall thin lady with spiky yellow hair. "Hello," she said, "I'm Mrs. Chumley-Smythe. Is Leopold here?"

"Leopold?" said Clarice.

"Who is Leopold?" asked Sadie.

Mrs. Chumley-Smythe said, "Leopold is my son."

Just then, Brick rode his bicycle up to the garden shed.

The thin lady's face broke into a fond smile. "Leo, dear, your cousin Jeremy and your Aunt Millicent and Uncle Toby will be coming at seven for dinner. So please don't be late." She bent and gave Brick a swift peck on the cheek. Then she started away.

Sadie said, "Mrs. Chumley-Smythe!"

Mrs. Chumley-Smythe turned and waited. "Yes, dear?"

"Is it true," said Sadie boldly, "that Brick — I mean Number Three — I mean Leopold — was raised in the African jungle? With animals?"

Mrs. Chumley-Smythe smiled fondly once again. "Indeed, yes. He was lost, but now he is found, aren't you, Leo dear?"

Brick squirmed with embarrassment.

"Where have I heard that before?" muttered Sadie.

Mrs. Chumley-Smythe waved her hand. "Seven o'clock, Leopold." Her voice was like a flute.

When she was gone, Sadie turned to Brick. "So your real name is Leopold Chumley-Smythe!"

Brick pulled a face and shuffled his feet.

"You said your name was Brick," accused Sadie.

Brick stared at the two girls with those unblinking amber eyes of his. Then his ears went back. "That's right," he said. "You want to make something of it?"

Sadie whispered to Clarice, "His ears moved!"

Clarice whispered back, "*Shshsh.*"

"His ears twitched back like a cat's," Sadie persisted, "I saw them."

Clarice waved a scrap of paper in the air. "Message in the coffee can from a kid named Holly Wren. Lives over on Larch Street. Asking us to find her budgie for her. She thinks it's been stolen by a local budgie-snatching ring."

"Missing budgie!" said Sadie in disgust. "Who

ever heard of a budgie-snatching ring! The kid hasn't lost her budgie, she's lost her marbles."

"We'd better get over there and interview her," said Clarice. "Bring your notebook, Number Two."

"Now?"

"Right now. Then on the way back we can go pick up Harinder Jay's bicycle for her."

"Who's Harinder Jay?" asked Sadie.

"Forgot to mention the second message," said Clarice waving a second scrap of paper. "She's a little kid lives on Willow. Her mother left this message asking us to find Harinder's stolen bike. It's a new bike too."

"And where do you suppose you're going to pick up Harinder's bike when you haven't even solved the crime yet?"

"That's easy. Bob Bream. Steals everyone's bike, remember? It'll be in the lane behind his house."

"You want I should punch him out, Chief?" said Brick.

"Won't be necessary, Number Three," said Clarice.

The three detectives set out for Larch Street. As they slouched along the seawall Brick pointed over at Isadora's restaurant. "Hey, there's Marmalade," he said.

"Where?" said Sadie.

"On the garbage bin," said Brick.

They stared.

"Got herself lost again," said Clarice. "Let's go take a look."

When they got closer, Sadie said, "It isn't Marmalade, it's the Varden cat."

"Ginger," said Brick.

"Here, Ginger, nice puss," called Clarice.

The cat recognized them. He arched his back and smiled. Brick reached up. Ginger collapsed gratefully into his arms and began to purr.

"We ought to take him back to the Vardens'," said Sadie.

Clarice considered. "Number Three will carry him. Should only take five minutes. Come on."

They hurried back up the Fairview hill. Clarice said, "They don't really deserve it. The Vardens are a pair of jerks. But for Ginger's sake . . . "

They reached the Vardens' back alley. Brick lifted Ginger up and placed him on top of the backyard wall. The cat gave a contented growl. He seemed happy to be home.

"G'bye, Ginger," purred Brick.

Suddenly, the backyard door burst open.

"You filthy cat thieves back again!"

It was Dolly Varden advancing on them like a wild elephant, waving her arms and screaming. "Herbert!" she screamed, "Herbert!"

"Run for it!" yelled Clarice.

They ran.

And didn't slow down to a walk until they were back down the hill at the seawall, out of breath and flushed with heat and excitement.

"Phew!" said Sadie. "That was close."

"Detective Work is Dangerous Work," said Clarice pompously. "Ginger is safely home even if there was no Thanks for it. But that's what being a Detective means; it's Lonely and it's Dirty and it's Thankless sometimes. Maybe that's why we do it. Someone has to. It's Tough and it's . . . "

Brick listened attentively.

Sadie, busy with her own thoughts, switched Clarice's voice off, but was soon jerked back to reality.

"Number Two, you're not listening."

"Sure, I'm listening," said Sadie, "what were you saying?"

"I was talking about the Report."

"What report?"

"The Case Report, of course. When you get it all written up I'll sign it. Makes it official. Then you can file it."

"Report? I've got to write a report? What report?"

"Our First Case, of course. We gotta keep a record of how we solved Miss Parsnip's cat problem. Write it up telling what I did and what you did and what Brick did, and what happened at Granville Market. And then you write — "

"You called him Brick."

Clarice glared. "If you would kindly stop interrupting . . ."

"But you called Number Three Brick."

"I called him Brick because we're not actually working on a Case right now."

"What about the case of the budgie-snatching ring? And what about the stolen bike?"

"We're not working on them yet. We got to accept a Case first. After the Client has been Interviewed. Anyway, do you want me to explain how to write up a Case Report?"

"No."

"Then write it."

They walked along in silence. Then Sadie said, "What shall I call it?"

"Call what?"

"The case."

"Call it what you like."

"Why then," said Sadie, "I'll call it 'The Witch of Crawley Mill.'"

"No you won't. Nobody over the age of six believes in witches. Call it 'The Case of the Marmalade Cat.'"